KNIT your BIT

A WORLD WAR I STORY

BY

DEBORAH HOPKINSON

ILLUSTRATED BY

STEVEN GUARNACCIA

G. P. Putnam's Sons • An Imprint of Penguin Group (USA) Inc.

WHEN Pop left to be a soldier,
I wanted to go with him.

"I'm brave," I told Pop.

"I know, Mikey," he said, patting my shoulder.
"And you'll need to be, 'cause it takes just as
much courage to stay behind."

Back home, Mama pulled out her knitting needles. "Our soldiers will be cold come winter."

"Teach me," Ellie begged. "I want to help."

"What about you, Mikey?" Mama asked, fishing out more needles.

"No way! Boys don't knit," I said. "Besides,
I want to do something *big* to help."

Ellie finished her first hat a few days later. It wasn't much to look at, but she wrapped it up to send to Pop right away. "You could knit him something, too, Mikey."

"Like I said, Sis, knitting is for girls."

"No, it's not," Ellie cried, grabbing the newspaper. "Everyone's helping. Look at these firemen. And even President Wilson keeps sheep on the White House lawn for wool."

Ellie turned the page:

"If we each do a little, it makes something big," she said.

I just rolled my eyes.

CENTRAL PARK

knitting

BEE

INDIVIDUAL & GROUP
SPEED KNITTING

PRIZES
FOR THE BEST

HATS SOCKS SCARVES

3 DAYS OF KNITTING
For our Soldiers in need

50¢ ENTRY FEE

A few days later, Miss Robin tacked a poster on the bulletin board.

"Wouldn't it be great if students from our class entered the Knitting Bee?" Miss Robin asked.

All the boys—including me—jeered.

"Mikey, you're always talking about how brave you are," Sarah said. "This is your chance to help. But I bet you're scared you can't learn."

"Me, scared? My friends and I can beat you any day."

"Mikey, sit down!" Nick hissed.

"Dare you to enter," the girls cried all together.

"It's a deal. Boys against girls. We'll call our team the . . . Boys' Knitting Brigade!" I thought that sounded big and important enough.

"Fine," said Josie. "We'll be the Purl Girls."

Purl Girls? I didn't even know what *purl* meant. I gulped. What had I gotten us into?

Mama offered to give us lessons.
Nick and Dan came over every day
after school to practice.

After we'd figured out how to hold our needles and knit,
which was hard enough, Mama even showed us how to purl.

Nick was the major of mufflers. I was the sergeant of socks
(which are not easy—believe me—especially the heels). As for
Dan, well, mostly his yarn just got tangled. (Our cat loved it.)

Finally, the day of the Knitting Bee arrived.

Central Park was a sea of women and men,

old and young—and lots and lots of girls.

"Forward march!" I commanded.

"Mikey, we're the only boys," whispered Nick.

"I sure hope we don't get laughed outta here."

"Look at that food! When do we eat?" Dan asked.

"Those sausages smell dee-licious."

"Over here, boys!" called Miss Robin.

Naturally, the Purl Girls were ready to go.

Sarah smiled sweetly, but she was all business. "Get ready to be beaten by the fastest knitters in New York City."

I led my troops to a nearby bench. "Ignore those girls, soldiers. Speed isn't everything. There are prizes for the best knitting, too."

We unraveled our yarn and grabbed our needles.
The band struck up a rousing march. Drummers
beat tin buckets—with knitting needles, of course.
Rat-tat-tat! Rat-tat-tat!

My men performed with courage (mostly).

Dan came close to deserting us for the food tables.
And Nick got distracted watching Mrs. Rizzo's flying
fingers. (She won a prize for knitting a sweater—five
hours and forty-five minutes exactly!)

We knit all afternoon, and the next day too.

By the third day, the pressure was on.

Dan's piece looked more like an old dishrag than a hat.

Nick was still clicking away, though the edges of his muffler were

all zigzaggy because he kept adding stitches or dropping them.

I'd finished one sock yesterday. Now I was on my second.

I was feeling pretty good. That first sock was definitely my best yet!

Maybe I'd even win a prize for the pair—if I could get the

second one done by the end of the day.

Ellie offered to bring me some lunch, but I just shook my head.

"Ooh, you're doing so good, Mikey. Let me see."

Ellie gave a little gasp. "Oh, no, Mikey. Look!" she whispered.

"A hole. You dropped a stitch right at the beginning there."

Somehow I'd missed it. But Ellie was right. To make it perfect,
I'd have to rip the whole sock apart and start over again.
I hung my head. Knitting was stupid.

I felt like breaking my needles and stomping on everything.

"Nice work, kid."

I glanced up.

A young soldier stood before me. He nodded toward my one perfect sock on the bench.

"Thank you, sir," I stammered.
I was still feeling miserable.
"But . . . I'm really not so good
at this."

"Well, you're trying, aren't
you? That's what counts."

We were silent a minute.

"You got someone over there?"

"Yes, sir. My dad," I told him.

All at once I missed Pop so much, my eyes stung. I wondered where he was. I could almost see him hiding in a muddy ditch, or shivering in the rain. How could anything I do—little or big—*really* help?

"Warm wool socks would've felt mighty cozy last winter," the soldier said. "So you keep on knitting, kid. I bet your dad will be real glad to wear those socks."

"Yes, sir." I wasn't sure what to do next, so I stood and saluted.

Then I took the sock apart and began again.

Needles Down!

Sarah had finished a muffler,
Molly had made a pair of socks,
and Josie's hat was perfect.

"Now let's see how *you* did," said Sarah.

For a minute we stood in silence.

Finally, Dan said, "I guess my yarn got a little greasy from the sausages."

We all laughed.

I held out my hand to Sarah. "You beat us fair and square."

"No hard feelings, Mikey?"

"Naw. Just wait till next time."

I never did finish that pair of Central Park Knitting Bee socks.

Instead, just before we left, I got up my courage and found the young soldier.

"This is for you." I held out my best-ever perfect sock.

"Gee, thanks, kid," he said. "And don't give up."

"I won't," I promised.

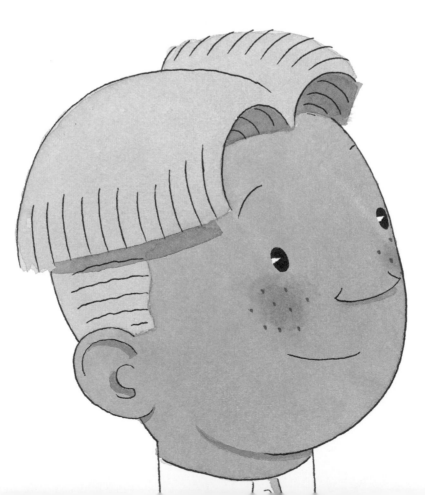

As for what happened after that, well,
Nick and Dan never went near knitting
needles again. But all by herself, Ellie
made hats for every soldier in Pop's unit.
They sent her a picture of themselves.

As for me, I did keep trying. And though it
took a while, I finally knit a pair of socks for Pop.
He wrote back to say they were his favorites.
He promised to wear them on the day he came home.

And he did.

AUTHOR'S NOTE

Knit Your Bit! is historical fiction inspired by real events.

When the United States entered World War I in April 1917, the American Red Cross determined that there were not enough warm sweaters, wool helmets, socks, mittens, and wristlets for soldiers in Europe to make it through the winter months. Knitting for soldiers during World War I therefore became a national effort by women, men, and children. This effort to "Knit for Sammy" (U.S. soldiers) spread across the country.

People started knitting clubs and knitting bees. They knit on subways and on their lunch hours, in classrooms and in church halls. Men and boys began knitting, too, from firemen in Honolulu, Hawaii, to the governor of Arizona. A group of schoolboys formed the Rocky Mountain Knitter Boys of Colorado, taking up their principal's challenge to be as patriotic as their girl classmates by knitting.

As part of this nationwide effort, on July 30, 1918, the Navy League Comforts Committee sponsored a three-day "Knit-In" at Central Park in New York City—the Central Park Knitting Bee of our story.

By all accounts, it was a fantastic success. *The New York Times* reported that the event raised $4,000. Mrs. Ethel Rizzo of East 67th Street, who completed an entire sweater in around six hours, won the prize for fastest knitter. Over the course of three days, volunteers knitted 50 sweaters, 48 mufflers, and 224 pairs of socks. Prize winners included four blind women, two men, an eighty-three-year-old woman, and four children under the age of eleven.

So what are you waiting for? Grab some needles and get knitting!

The nation's spirit of cooperation is reflected in the following song, printed in the *Seattle School Bulletin* in May 1918:

Johnnie, get your yarn, get your yarn, get your yarn;
Knitting has a charm, has a charm, has a charm;
See us knitting two by two,
Boys in Seattle like it too.
Hurry every day, don't delay, make it pay.
Our laddies must be warm, not forlorn mid the storm.
Hear them call from o'er the sea,
"Make a sweater, please, for me."
Over here everywhere,
We are knitting for the boys over there;
It's a sock or a sweater, or even better,
To do your bit and knit a square.

YOU CAN STILL KNIT YOUR BIT!

Knitting for soldiers overseas
continues to this day.
Visit with your local yarn store or
knitting guild to find a group in your area.
Or check out the following websites:

Knit Your Bit at the National World War II Museum in New Orleans
http://www.nationalww2museum.org/learn/knit-your-bit/index.html

Knitting for Charity
http://www.knittingforcharity.org/

For Vicki Hemphill, Robin Smith,

Ellie Thomas, and Deborah Wiles,

four wonderful knitters—and friends. —D.H.

For Mom —S.G.

LEARN MORE

"Knitting for Victory—World War I" by Paula Becker (HistoryLink.org Essay 5721)
http://www.historylink.org/index.cfm?DisplayPage=output.cfm&File_Id=5721
(Source for *Seattle School Bulletin* knitting song on previous page)

American Red Cross Museum—historic knitting patterns
http://www.redcross.org/museum/exhibits/knits.asp

G. P. PUTNAM'S SONS • A division of Penguin Young Readers Group.
Published by The Penguin Group.
Penguin Group (USA) Inc., 375 Hudson Street, New York, NY 10014, U.S.A.
Penguin Group (Canada), 90 Eglinton Avenue East, Suite 700, Toronto, Ontario M4P 2Y3, Canada (a division of Pearson Penguin Canada Inc.).
Penguin Books Ltd, 80 Strand, London WC2R 0RL, England.
Penguin Ireland, 25 St. Stephen's Green, Dublin 2, Ireland (a division of Penguin Books Ltd).
Penguin Group (Australia), 250 Camberwell Road, Camberwell, Victoria 3124, Australia (a division of Pearson Australia Group Pty Ltd).
Penguin Books India Pvt Ltd, 11 Community Centre, Panchsheel Park, New Delhi - 110 017, India.
Penguin Group (NZ), 67 Apollo Drive, Rosedale, Auckland 0632, New Zealand (a division of Pearson New Zealand Ltd).
Penguin Books (South Africa) (Pty) Ltd, 24 Sturdee Avenue, Rosebank, Johannesburg 2196, South Africa.
Penguin Books Ltd, Registered Offices: 80 Strand, London WC2R 0RL, England.

Design by Marikka Tamura. Text set ITC Usherwood Std.
The art for this book was drawn with pen and ink, and then painted with watercolors.
Library of Congress Cataloging-in-Publication Data
Hopkinson, Deborah.
Knit your bit : a World War I story / by Deborah Hopkinson ; illustrated by Steven Guarnaccia.   p. cm.
Summary: When Mikey's father leaves to fight in World War I, he and his classmates join
the Central Park Knitting Bee to help knit clothing for soldiers overseas.
1. World War, 1914–1918—New York (State)—New York—Fiction. [1. World War, 1914–1918—United States—Fiction.
2. Knitting—Fiction. 3. Sex role—Fiction. 4. New York (N.Y.)—History—1898–1951—Fiction.] I. Guarnaccia, Steven, ill. II. Title.
PZ7.H778125Kn 2013   [Fic]—dc23   2012009635
ISBN 978-0-399-25241-9
1 3 5 7 9 10 8 6 4 2

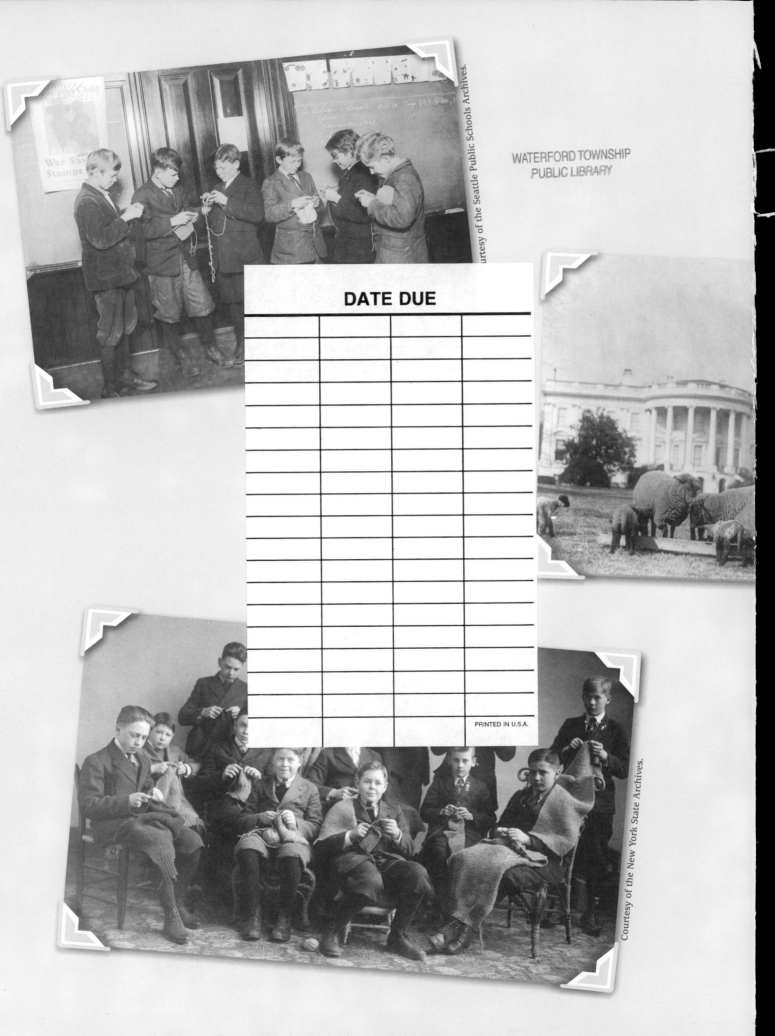

DATE DUE

PRINTED IN U.S.A.